AF349308

ISBN: 978-88-31314-47-3
©℗ 2020 Pietro Favorito
cuorenoiredizioni@gmail.com

Creating Mind: Pietro Favorito
Art: Enzo Di Lauro
Lettering: Domenico Nagliero
General Counsel and translate: Erika Pace

Hot Play

Central Park, Brindisi. The first night of Autumn is falling and a scaring woman is wondering among the trees in the park.
"I'M EVIL, AND DANGEROUS."
"VERY DANGEROUS."
"I'M NOT ALIVE, OR DEAD. AND THE COLD RUNNING THROUGH MY VEINS FREEZES MY BODY AND TEARS MY FLESH."
"MY NAME IS GIADA, AND I'M DAMMED TO THE ENDLESS PAIN, THE ULTIMATE SUFFER. BECAUSE I LOVE LIFE. BECAUSE I LOVE THE WARMTH. BECAUSE I LOVE MY MAN."

"EVERY NIGHT IN THE DARK I LOOK FOR A PEACE THAT I CAN'T FIND."
"I NEED BLOOD. A LOT OF IT."
"SO I WON'T BE COLD. SO I WON'T BE OFF.
SO I WON'T BE ARID."

"I STEAL LIVES TO BE ALIVE."

"TO EASE THE PAIN."

"PAIN MAKES YOU EVIL."
"ON THE OTHER HAND, LOVE..."
"... MAKES YOU RUTHLESS."

"IT MAKES YOU MAD!"
DRIIIN! DRIIIN!
FINALLY MY LOVE!

"PLEASE, MAKE ME YOURS LIKE NEVER BEFORE!"
"THIS IS GOING TO BE OUR LAST TIME TOGETHER."
"YOU DESERVE LIFE. I CAN GIVE YOU BUT DEATH INSTEAD. I WON'T DAMN YOU TO HELL, EVEN THOUGH IT WILL BE WORST FOR ME THERE WITHOUT YOU."

"BE HAPPY, MY LOVE. AND FORGIVE ME, IF YOU CAN!"

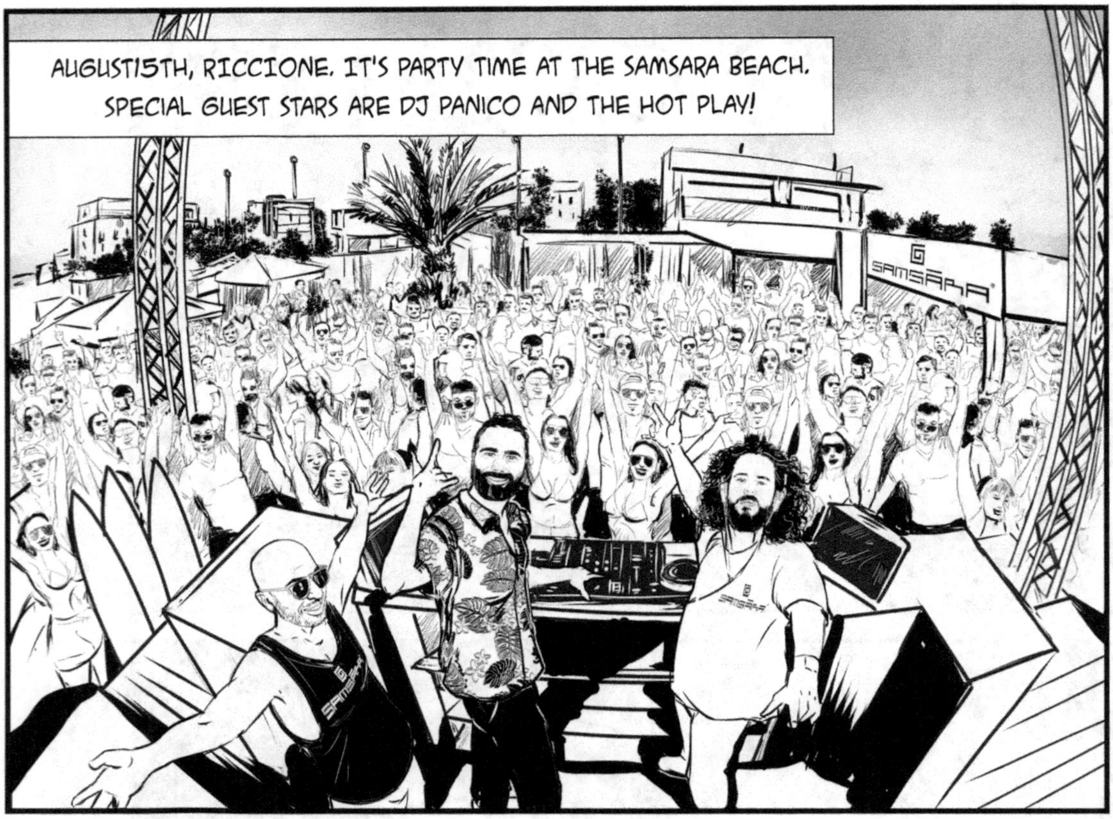

AUGUST15TH, RICCIONE. IT'S PARTY TIME AT THE SAMSARA BEACH. SPECIAL GUEST STARS ARE DJ PANICO AND THE HOT PLAY!
LET'S CHECK ON PETER AND KLAUS! IT LOOKS LIKE THE HOTPLAY DON'T FEEL LIKE PERFORMING TONIGHT!

ROCCO... DAVID... JOIN US! WE ARE CELEBRATING PETER AND CHRISTINA, MY LITTLE SISTER. THEY ARE FINALLY ENGAGED!
SAMSARA

WOW, CONGRATS, GUYS!
SAMSARA
YOUR PARTNER IS A LUCKY MAN! CRISTINA IS WONDERFUL!
SAMSARA

I DON'T KNOW ABOUT THE LUCKY PART... MARRYING MY SISTER, PETER ENDS UP UNDER MY CONTROL!!! HE WILL HAVE TO PROPERLY BEHAVE OR ELSE!

WE ARE HERE WAITING FOR CELEBRATING BUT THE TWO LOVEBIRDS SEEM TO HAVE DISAPPEARED.

KLAUS, I HAVE TO ASK YOU THIS: ARE YOU SURE YOU AND CHRISTINA ARE SIBLINGS? YOU KNOW, CHRISTINA IS PRETTY AND BRIGHT... AND YOU ARE NOT!

LEAVE MY BEST MAN ALONE, GUYS! DON'T GIVE HIM AN EXCUSE TO GIVE ME THE WORST WEDDING PRESENT EVER!
SAMSARA

WE JUST LEARNED ABOUT YOUR ENGAGEMENT. WHEN EXACTLY ARE YOU GETTING MARRIED?
ROCCO, WHENEVER IT IS, THEY MUST CELEBRATE HERE AT SAMSARA BEACH... OTHERWISE THE HOT PLAY WON'T GET A PENNY FOR THEIR PERFORMANCE TONIGHT!
SAMSARA
DAVID, THAT'S ON YOU THEN... IN EXACTLY ONE YEAR FROM TODAY WE WILL BE HERE ALL TOGETHER AGAIN! INCLUDING KLAUS... FOR EVERYONE'S JOY!
WOULD YOU PLEASE STOP TEASING MY BROTHER! IT'S NOT HIS FAULT IF HE IS THE WAY HE IS!

KLAUS, LISTEN TO ME... GO AND PLAY SOME MUSIC... LET'S GET THE PARTY STARTED!

I'M COMING! FINALLY IT'S TIME FOR SOME HOT PLAY STYLE FUN!
SAMSARA

I'M COMING! FINALLY IT'S TIME FOR SOME HOT PLAY STYLE FUN!

BITCH!

DON'T FORGET PANIC, PLAY A SONG WITH A LONG INTRO... DAVID IS GOING TO INTRODUCE THE HOT PLAY!!!

CAN I BUY YOU A DRINK AT LEAST, SINCE YOU NO LONGER RETURN MY CALLS?
MICHELE, OUR RELATIONSHIP ENDED TWO YEARS AGO. WHY DON'T YOU GET IT? YOU HAVE TO LET IT GO. I DON'T WANT TO SEE YOU ANYMORE!

CRISTINA, DON'T GO! COME BACK! YOU CAN'T TREAT ME LIKE THIS!

CICCIORICCIO IS A CULT RADIO IN BRINDISI, ONE OF THE MOST LISTENED TO IN SOUTHERN ITALY.
A MONTH LATER...
CICCIORICCIO IS ALSO THE RADIO THAT BROADCASTS THE HOT PLAY PROGRAM DEDICATED TO DANCE MUSIC EVERY EVENING.
Ciccio Riccio
1983
RADIO CICCIORICCIO!

AND AFTER AN EVENING OF GREAT MUSIC, LET'S CLOSE WITH ONE LAST SONG FOR TODAY...

...OUR EMPATHY ... THE FIRST SINGLE SIGNED BY HOT PLAY! UNTIL NEXT TIME, THEN FRIENDS. GREETINGS FROM PETER AND KLAUS!
Ciccio
1983
Riccio

THIS IS ALSO GONE, AND THE RADIO LISTENERS HAVE INTERACTED IN MANY, PLENTY OF MESSAGES ON OUR FACEBOOK PAGE... WHAT ELSE CAN WE ASK FOR?
I CAN'T SPEAK FOR YOU GUYS, BUT I REALLY FEEL LIKE TAKING A WALK ON THE WATERFRONT!
IT'S NOT EXACTLY WHAT I WAS THINKING ABOUT, BUT IN ORDER TO SATISFY MY SHINING STAR I'M READY FOR ANY SACRIFICE.
ARE YOU GOING, BROTHER?
NO WAY! THE SKY IS CLOUDING OVER. LOOK AT THE MOON, IT'S ALMOST COMPLETELY COVERED. IN MY OPINION, IT WILL RAIN IN A LITTLE WHILE.

IGNORE IT, LOVE. TONIGHT, YOU'LL SEE, IT WON'T RAIN. I LOVE YOU TOO MUCH FOR IT TO HAPPEN.
I TRUST YOUR INSTINCTS, CRISTINA ... AS ALWAYS. AND ANYWAY, EVEN IF THE UNIVERSAL FLOOD CAME, I WOULDN'T NOTICE ANYTHING WITH YOU BY MY SIDE!

I DON'T WANT TO SOUND PESSIMISTIC TO YOU, BUT IF WE DON'T HURRY BACK TO THE CAR, WE'LL TAKE OUR FIRST OUTDOOR SHOWER! NOW IT'S JUST YOU AND ME WALKING ON THE WATERFRONT.

DON'T WORRY, MY FRIEND... YOU ARE NOT ALONE !!!

SO, YOU PIECE OF SHIT, DID YOU AND CRISTINA HAVE A GOOD TIME BEHIND MY BACK? DID YOU LAUGH AT ME?

YOU SHOULDN'T HAVE CHEATED ON ME... IT WASN'T REALLY NICE OF YOU.

OUR STORY WAS ALREADY OVER. YOU AND I WERE TOGETHER ONLY IN YOUR IMAGINATION. I LEFT YOU, AND YOU SIMPLY DIDN'T ACCEPTED IT. EXACTLY HOW YOU DON'T ACCEPT IT NOW!

IT WILL NEVER BE OVER BETWEEN US UNTIL I SAY SO. YOU STILL LOVE ME ... YOU NEVER STOPPED!
DON'T YOU DARE TOUCH HER!

BE SILENT!
I'M NOT TALKING
TO YOU!

LET GO OF MY HAND IMMEDIATELY! THEN SIT ON THE GROUND, AND ENJOY THE SHOW. YOU MADE A SLUT OF THIS WOMAN, AND NOW SHE WILL BE TREATED LIKE ONE!
MICHELE, LOWER THAT WEAPON... WHAT'S WRONG WITH YOU, ARE YOU CRAZY?

AM I CRAZY??? WHAT A GOOD QUESTION! DO YOU REALLY WANT AN ANSWER? DO YOU REALLY WANT TO KNOW HOW CRAZY I AM ?
MICHELE... PLEASE... LOWER...

STUMP!
SHUT UP!!!!

BANG!

NOOOOOOO!!!!
BANG!
PETEEEEEEER!!!

BASTARD!!!!!!!!!!!!

OH YES, DARLING. I'M A BASTARD. A HUGE BASTARD.

LET'S GET THE PARTY STARTED, GUYS! CRISTINA NEEDS TO FORGET THIS BAD EVENING!
YOU ARE NOT A MAN ... YOU ARE JUST A LOOSER! I HATE YOU! I HATE YOU SO MUCH !!!

WHAT THE FUCK ARE YOU LOOKING AT?
NOOOOOOOO!!!!
PETEEEEEEER!!!
STUMP!

IN THAT VERY MOMENT...
NOOOOOOO!!! PETEEEEEEER?!!!!

IT CAN'T BE TRUE! NO, IT CAN'T BE TRUE!!

MY - DEAR - LOVE- NOOOO!!!!

"HOLD ON, MY LOVE...
PLEASE, DON'T DIE!"

"I SACRIFICED OUR LOVE FOR YOUR HAPPINESS... IT CAN'T END LIKE THIS."
"I WON'T LET IT END LIKE THIS."

EVERYTHING'S FINE, MY LOVE. LOOK AT ME, I'M STANDING AND I'M COMING TO YOU.

YOU... YOU CAN STAND UP, CAN'T YOU? WE HAVE TO GO HOME... IT'S LATE.

I KNOW, YOU DON'T LOOK GOOD RIGHT NOW, BUT YOU'RE STRONG AND YOU'LL RECOVER. IT'S ONLY A MATTER OF TIME...

UUUHEEEEEE
THE SIRENS! I CAN HEAR THEM! THEY ARE HERE, WE ARE SAFE!
BUT SAY SOMETHING... MOVE AN ARM... GIVE ME A SIGN...
LET ME UNDERSTAND THAT I'M NOT WRONG...
I'M CALLING 911 AND THEY WILL SEND AN AMBULANCE. YOU JUST PROMISE ME YOU WON'T GIVE UP... BECAUSE... I CAN'T LIVE WITHOUT YOU.
HOW ARE YOU, MADAM? ARE YOU HURT? WHAT HAPPENED?
BEASTS, SOME BEASTS... SHUT MY FIANCE... THEN THEY BEAT ME BEFORE TAKING ME OVER THERE AND...
PETER, TAKE CARE OF PETER!!! I'M FINE!!!!

LET ME GO, LET ME GO! I HAVE TO GET TO HIM !!!

AND TAKE OFF THIS UMBRELLA! I WANT RAIN TO WASH MY BODY! LET THE WATER PURIFY MY SOUL!

I WANT TO BE PURE ... FOR MY LOVE. WE HAVE TO GET MARRIED! PETEEEEER!
I'M GIVING HER A SEDATIVE, THE GIRL IS IN A STATE OF SHOCK.

I HAVE TO BE PURE... I HAVE TO BE PURE... PURE... PURE...

HOW IS CRISTINA, KLAUS?
SHE'S DEVASTATED. THEY KEEP HER UNDER SEDATION ... SHE IS SLEEPING RIGHT NOW.
VISITE

WHAT CAN YOU TELL US ABOUT PETER?
DOCTORS ARE DOING THE IMPOSSIBLE ...

BUT A DEAR FRIEND OF MINE, WHO IS AMONG THE DOCTORS WHO ARE TAKING CARE OF HIM, MADE ME UNDERSTAND THAT THERE IS NO HOPE...
...NOW ONLY A MIRACLE IS NEEDED!

POOR PETER, HE DIDN'T DESERVE SUCH A FATE.
AND CRISTINA? NOT ONLY THE VIOLENCE...
CURSED THE DAY HE MET THAT MONSTER OF HER EX BOYFRIEND...

I DIDN'T MEET ANYONE. MICHELE DOESN'T EXIST...

HE NEVER EXISTED... IF I NO LONGER EXIST.

CRISTINA!!!

MY GOD, CRISTINA? CRISTINAAAAA?!?!?!

THERE IS PAIN ONLY WHERE THERE IS LIFE.
CRISTINA, NO!!!

AND TERRIBLE IS THE THOUGHT OF HAVING TO LIVE WITHOUT PETER...

NOOOOOOOO!
STUMP!

A FLOWER AMONG THE FLOWERS

Life will be only when I see you again
Shining like a precious diamond
 I will breathe your pure and wonderful soul
as it happens in all my dreams.
There is no thought that I do not dedicate to you
And that pain that grows more and more every day
I can never stop, it's like the weather
That flows violently towards my nightmare.

A flower among the flowers
You are a flower among the flowers
The most beautiful one
Who spoke to the moon
While the stars smiled at you
You are a flower among the flowers
Blossomed in the night
And kissed by a sun
Which no longer shines.

 Love will only be when I remember you
Because love can never die
I used to read it in your eyes every day
When I stared at you and mirrored myself in you
You walked silently by my side
yet the things you told me were endless
Our hearts beat together
At the rhythm of two lives becoming one
You are a flower among the flowers
The most beautiful one
Who spoke to the moon
While the stars smiled at you
You are a flower among the flowers
Blossomed in the night
And kissed by a sun
Which no longer shines.

MICHELE, CRISTINA IS DEAD!!! IT'S OUR FAULT!!! I DON'T WANT TO GO TO JAIL!
A FEW MONTHS LATER...

NOBODY WILL GO TO JAIL! FIRST OF ALL CRISTINA COMMITTED SUICIDE. SECOND... THE LAWYER SAYS THERE IS NOT ENOUGH EVIDENCE FOR AN INDICTMENT. THE DNA SAMPLES WERE HEAVILY CONTAMINATED BY THE RAIN AND THEREFORE MATCHES ARE MINIMAL!

WHAT ABOUT PETER... WHAT HAPPENED TO HIM? HE DISAPPEARED FROM THE HOSPITAL... NOBODY HAS HEARD OF HIM. I CAN'T HELP IT... I'M AFRAID!
MICHELE, ROOSTER IS RIGHT. WE SHOULD DO SOMETHING!

DO WHAT? HUNT A GHOST WITH A BULLET IN THE FOREHEAD ???
PETER IS DEAD... AND SOMEONE MUST HAVE STOLEN HIS BODY TO CAUSE TROUBLE.
TO SCARE US OR WHATSOEVER! BUT REST ASSURED... I WILL SOON FIND OUT WHAT HAPPENED.

PLEASE, MICHELE... YOU HAVE TO DO SOMETHING ABOUT IT. I'M TERRIFIED.

I'LL FIX EVERYTHING, RUSTER. AS ALWAYS. HAS YOUR CAPTAIN EVER LET YOU DOWN BEFORE?
NO... YOU'VE NEVER LET US DOWN!

CRAAAK!

ONCE, EVIL NIGHT, YOU WERE THE QUEEN...
...AND BETWEEN MUSIC AND SEX YOU SHONE DIVINELY.
CRAAK!

IT IS RAINING... AND THUNDERING...
YES, LIKE THAT DAMMED EVENING THAT RUINED OUR LIVES.

ONCE, DARK TEACHER, YOU WERE THE STRONGEST, BUT THEN I DEFEATED YOU, I MET DEATH.
FROM THAT SAD MOMENT I RULE YOUR KINGDOM... WET WITH THE BLOOD I LEAVE AS MY SIGN.

WE SHOULDN'T HAVE LISTENED TO HIM. MICHELE AND HIS BULLSHIT PUT US IN A SEA O F...
TUMP!!!
CRASCH!
SHIT! WHAT WAS THAT?
AAAAAAHHHHHH!!!!
DEMON, HELP ME!!!! DO SOMETHING... I'M LOSING CONTROL!!!!!

NO WAY! YOU WERE DEAD!!! YOU'RE NOT HUMAN... WHO THE FUCK ARE YOU?!?!?

A DANCER! AND NOW I'LL MAKE YOU DANCE WITH ME BETWEEN LIFE AND DEATH!

WAS IT FUN TO TAKE ADVANTAGE OF A POOR WOMAN WHO WAS CRYING FOR HER LOVE? DID YOU LIKE IT? DID YOU ENJOY IT?
AAAAHHHHHH!!

YOU WILL BLEED TO DEATH, ASSHOLE??? OR CAN'T YOU BREATHE ALREADY? WELL, ONE WAY OR ANOTHER, YOU'LL DIE A TERRIBLE DEATH!!!

WHERE ARE YOU GOING, COWARD???

LET ME BE...
I DIDN'T MEAN TO...

I DON'T MEAN EITHER... BUT BELIEVE IT, I MUST!!!

AAAAAAAAAHHHHHHHH!!!!!
DEMON!!!!

THERE'S NOTHING YOU CAN DO AGAINST THIS BITE OF MINE. THERE'S NO REMEDY OR ANTIDOTE. IN THIS BITE THERE IS ALL THE POISON OF MONTHS OF PAIN...

A PAIN THAT LITTLE BY LITTLE WILL EAT YOUR BODY. IT WILL BECOME ROTTEN, AND YOUR SUFFER UNIMAGINABLE.

GO BACK TO YOUR FRIENDS. COME BACK TO YOUR BOSS. AND SHOW HIM YOUR SPECTACULAR END!

ONE LAST COURTESY... TELL THOSE BASTARDS THAT SOON PETER WILL VISIT THEM! THAT THEY SHOULD GET READY TO DIE!

THAT SAME NIGHT, LIKE ALL NIGHTS AT THAT SAME TIME, KLAUS IS THERE, WHERE THE NIGHTMARE KNEW HIS DARKEST POINT.
PRONTO SOCCORSO

I SHOULD HAVE COME WITH YOU. ALL THIS WOULD NOT HAVE HAPPENED. FORGIVE ME, MY SISTER!
CRISTINA DOCUPIL FOREVER IN OUR HEARTS.

THERE ARE NO GOOD NEWS. IT SEEMS THAT MICHELE AND HIS FRIENDS WILL GET AWAY WITH IT. BUT I WON'T GIVE UP. I WILL FIGHT UNTIL I HAVE BREATH FOR YOU TO GET JUSTICE.

NOW I HAVE TO GO, AND UNLESS PETER IS ALREADY WITH YOU, I'LL SEND HIM YOUR GREETINGS... WHEREEVER HE IS.

WHAT SADNESS THAT EMPTY HOUSE... WHERE ARE YOU, MY FRIEND? WHERE ARE...

NO, IT CANNOT BE! I SEE A LIGHT!!!

I WAS WAITING FOR YOU, COME ON UP!
PETER!!!

PETER IS BACK!!!
AND HE'S OK!!! MY GOD, IF
THIS IS A DREAM, PLEASE DO
NOT WAKE ME UP!

COME HERE AND HUG ME,
BROTHER!!! DAMNED, WHAT HAVE YOU DONE?
WHERE HAVE YOU BEEN? THE DOCTORS SAID
YOU NEEDED A MIRACLE, YOU KNOW? THEN
YOU DISAPPERED LEAVEING NO TRACE...
NOTHING... AND NOW...

AND NOW
I'M HERE.

YES, YOU ARE HERE NOW. I CAN'T BELIEVE
MY EYES... YOU DON'T LOOK VERY GOOD THOUGH.
WHAT HAPPENED TO YOU? HOW IS IT POSSIBLE THAT
YOU CAN MOVE... TALK, BREATHE WITHOUT THE HELP
OF THE MACHINES... I MEAN, WELL, YOU KNOW WHAT
I MEAN... HOW IS IT POSSIBLE THAT YOU
ARE STILL ALIVE?

YOU'RE WRONG, KLAUS,
I AM NOT ALIVE. AND MAYBE NEITHER ARE YOU.
OUR LIVES CAN NO LONGER BE CALLED LIVES WITHOUT
CRISTINA. AND YOU JUST ASKED ME TO TELL YOU THE
TRUTH... BUT I CAN'T ANSWER YOU!
HOW THE HELL COULD I?!?!?
ABOUT ONE THING YOU WERE RIGHT THOUGH. THERE WAS NO HOPE
FOR ME! I WAS PRACTICALLY DEAD. JUST ONE MORE SMALL STEP AND
I WOULD HAVE LEFT THIS WORLD FOREVER...
HI, DJ!
I DON'T ASK YOU HOW YOU'RE
DOING BECAUSE I KNOW EXACTLY
THAT NOTHING WORSE THAN THIS
COULD HAVE EVER HAPPENED TO
YOU... LIFE CAN BE SO
UNFAIR SOMETIMES!

I RAN AWAY FROM YOU NOT TO DRAG YOU IN THE IMMENSE PAIN OF MY HELL... AND NOW TO TAKE YOU AWAY FROM THE DEATH, I HAVE NO OTHER CHOICE THAN TO MAKE YOU HIS ALLIED!
YOU CANNOT END UP LIKE THIS, IT'S NOT FAIR! AND EVEN IF I HAVE NO IDEA OF WHAT YOU REALLY WANT... I WON'T LET YOU LIVE LIKE A VEGETABLE IN A HOSPITAL'S BED FOR THE REST OF YOUR DAYS!!!
FORGIVE ME IF I TAKE YOU WITH ME... BUT I STILL LOVE YOU... I NEVER STOPPED. AND WITH THIS KISS I ASK YOU FOR FORGIVENESS!

KING OF HELL, LORD OF DEATH AND EVIL, HERE I AM TO GIVE YOU MY GREATEST LOVE IN HIS HUMAN FORM: RELEASE IT FROM THE LIGHT AND LEAD IT TO ETERNAL DARKNESS. I AM STEALING HIS SOUL TO OFFER IT AS A GIFT TO YOU!

I THINK IT WAS A MIRACLE, BRO! I OPENED MY EYES AND I WAS ALIVE. I DIDN'T REMEMBER ANYTHING... I HAD LOST MY MEMORY. SO I STARTED TO WANDER IN THE NIGHT... AND FROM THAT MOMENT I HAVE NEVER STOPPED UNTIL MY MEMORY HAS RETURNED...

AND THEN IT WAS TERRIBLE! REALLY TERRIBLE!!!

I WROTE SOMETHING THINKING ABOUT CRISTINA... TURN IT INTO MUSIC... THE MOST BEAUTIFUL AND SUBLIME OF ALL, AND SEND THE SONG TO THE PRODUCER SIMONE FIORI OF THE S-RECORDS... YOU WILL SEE THAT THIS TIME HE WILL LEND US A HAND.

A FEW DAYS LATER, WHILE KLAUS IS STILL IN THE RECORDING STUDIO TO MUSIC THE TEXT WRITTEN BY PETER...

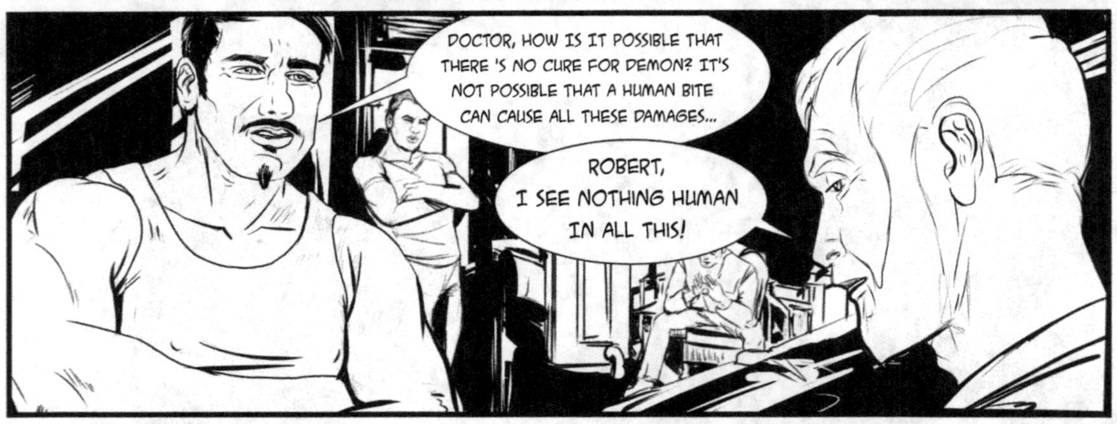

AND NOW FORGIVE ME, DEMON... I DO IT FOR YOU!

DON'T SHOOT... NO ONE TOLD YOU THAT THAT WORM MUST STOP SUFFERING!!!

OH MY GOD, HE HAS FOUND US... THAT DEVIL HAS FOUND US!!!

LEAVE, DOCTOR. THIS HAS NOTHING TO DO WITH YOU... SOON THERE WILL BE ONLY DEATH AND BLOOD IN HERE!!!

HERE THERE WILL BE ONLY ONE DEAD MAN... AND THAT IS YOU!!!
BANG!

AUCH!!!

SORRY, ROBERT, BUT YOU CANNOT KILL THE SAME MAN TWICE.
I DIDN'T TOUCH HER!!! NOT EVEN WITH A FINGER...

BUT YOU WERE THERE, AND I HEARD YOU LAUGHING, INSULTING HER... HUMILIETING HER... YOU FELT STRONG, DIDN'T YOU?

WHAT ELSE COULD I DO? MICHELE ... AAAAHHH
SHUT UP!!! I SHOULD CONDEMN YOU TO LIVE IN ETERNAL FEAR, BUT YOU DON'T DESERVE IT!!!

BANG!
BANG!

YOU CANNOT KILL A DEAD MAN!!!

BUT THE DEAD MAN CAN KILL YOU!!!

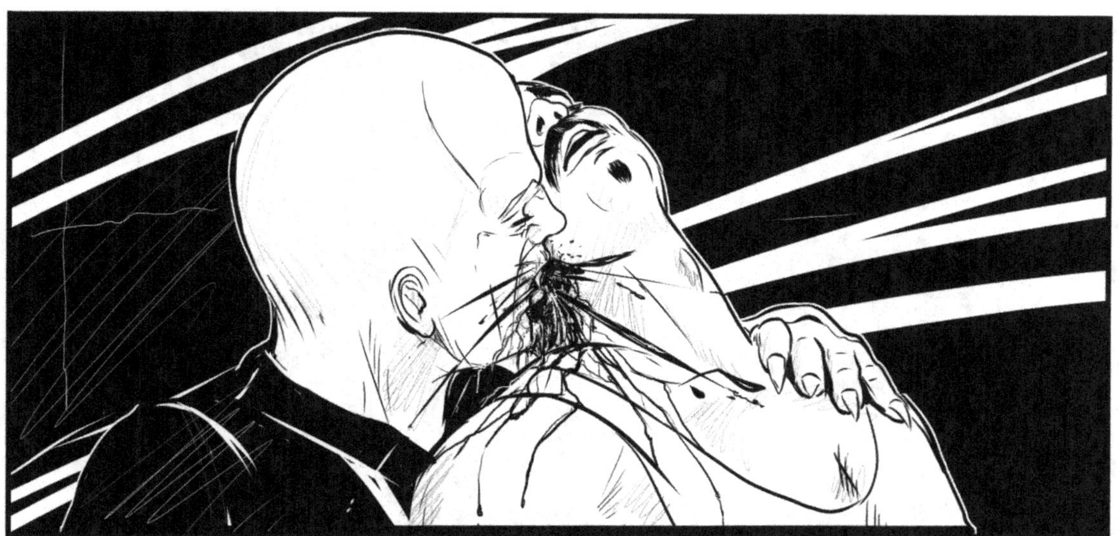

ONCE UPON A TIME THERE WERE FIVE HIDEUS PEOPLE, FIVE COWARDS WHO FOLLOWED A HAPPY COUPLE TO SHATTER THEIR DREAMS, TO DESTROY THEIR LIVES.

ONE AND ONLY ONE OF THEM WAS MOVED BY HATE AND JEALOUSY ...

THE OTHERS WERE JUST FOOLS THAT WANTED TO ENJOY THEMSELVES!!

THEY THOUGHT THEY ORGANIZED A PARTY!!! THEY THOUGHT THAT FOR THE REST OF THEIR DAYS THEY WOULD LAUGH REMEMBERING THE EVIL THAT THEY DID TO THAT COUPLE ...

WHO'S LAUGHING NOW THOUGH? NO ONE, EXCEPT THE DEATH!!!
CRACK!!!

NOOOOO!!!
OOOOO!!!
PLEASE DON'T!!!!
EEEEE
LEAVE ME ALONE!!!
EEE
PLEEEEEEEEEEEEEEEE...
THE MOST BEAUTIFUL MOMENTS LIVED TOGETHER ARE STILL THERE, BEFORE MY EYES!
YET, IT'S SOMETHING ELSE THAT I HEAR...
SHOTS AND... YOUR DESPERATE SCREAMS!
YOU CRY, SUFFER, AND BEG FOR THE HORROR TO STOP.
BUT IT DOESN'T.
THEY LAUGH AT YOU, THEY HARMED YOU SO BADLY...
AND THERE'S NOTHING I CAN DO FOR YOU! NOTHING!!!

...TODAY WAS THE FUNERALS DAY OF THREE MEN WELL KNOWN TO THE LOCAL POLICE. THEY HAD BEEN FOUND BARBARICALLY KILLED IN A GROUND FLOOR APPARTMENT IN THE HISTORICAL CENTER OF BRINDISI. UNTIL NOW THE INVESTIGATIONS HAVE LED TO NOTHING RELEVANT, EXCEPT THAT ALL OF THE MURDERED MEN WERE INVOLVED IN THE TRAGIC EVENT OF CRISTINA DOCUPIL'S SUICIDE!!!
IT WAS YOU, PETER... I KNOW IT!!! BUT WHY KEEPING ME AWAY FROM EVERYTHING??? I WOULD HAVE DONE ANYTHING TO HELP YOU... CRISTINA WAS MY SISTER !!! YOU DID THE WHOLE THING BY YOURSELF AND THEN YOU DISAPPEARED AGAIN...
DRINN!!
HELLO KLAUS, I AM SIMONE FIORI OF S-RECORDS AND I AM VERY HAPPY TO INFORM YOU THAT THE HOTPLAYS WILL BE PART OF MY MUSICAL LABEL. I HAVE BIG PLANS FOR YOU ...

...AND THE FACT THAT YOUR SONG WILL BE PLAYED BY ALL NATIONAL RADIOS IS NOT EVEN THE MOST EXCITING NEWS I HAVE TO GIVE YOU.
RECORDS
THERE'S A BIG PHONE COMPANY THAT WANTS THE SONG FOR A TELEVISION SPOT! YOU ARE GOING TO EXPLODE!!!

THAT'S WHY THERE'S NO TIME TO LOSE. YOU HAVE TO WORK ON A NEW SONG ALREADY! SERIOUS PROGRAMMING IS NEEDED... TO RIDE THE WAVE OF SUCCESS !!!
I CAN'T BELIEVE IT, MY DREAM COMES TRUE... CRISTINA... FROM UP THERE... YOU ARE HELPING US... THERE'S NO OTHER EXPLANATION. YET IT'S PETER NOW THAT NEEDS YOU THE MOST. I BELIEVE HE'S IN BIG TROUBLE.

IN THAT VERY MOMENT...
DOCTOR, WHAT YOU ARE SAYING... A VAMPIRE? DO YOU REALLY WANT ME TO BELIEVE IN THE EXISTENCE OF VAMPIRES ???

I KNOW EXACTLY WHAT I SAW, AND UNLESS YOU WANT TO DIE, YOU BETTER LISTEN TO ME: THAT THING HAS BEEN SPAT OUT OF HELL! NO BULLSHIT... UNLIKE THE POPULAR BELIEFS THAT BELIEVE IN STOPPING VAMPIRES WITH A CRUCIFIX, GARLIC, OR PUTTING A WOODEN POLE IN THEIR HEARTS.

WE ARE TALKING ABOUT CREATURES WITH A SUPERHUMAN FORCE, PROTECTED BY SATAN HIMSELF!!! HIRE BODY GUARDS, PHYSICALLY STRONG AND FEARLESS... VAMPIRES FEED THEMSELVES FROM HUMAN FEAR, WHICH GIVE THEM EXTRORDINARY STRENGTH.

IF YOU WANT TO GET RID OF HIM, YOU MUST DESTROY ITS BODY. YOU MUST BURN ITS HEAD IN ONE PLACE AND ITS HEART IN ANOTHER. YOU MUST SPREAD ITS ASHES EVERYWHERE, SO THAT THEY WON'T COME BACK TOGETHER. I DON'T KNOW HOW, BUT YOU HAVE TO FIND IT... BEFORE THAT THING FINDS YOU!!!
I KNOW HOW!

MEANWHILE, IN THAT CURSED PLACE...
UNDER A HEAVY RAIN THAT CAN'T HIDE NEITHER TEARS OR BLOOD...
I WAS SURE I WOULD FIND YOU HERE!!!

YOU HAD NO RIGHTS! AND STOP LOOKING FOR ME... I DON'T WANT TO SEE YOU EVER AGAIN!!!

I HAD NO CHOICE, PETER !!! I LOST YOU ONCE... BUT AT LEAST YOU WERE HAPPY WITH CRISTINA... I COULDN'T LOSE YOU AGAIN... FOREVER... I LOVE YOU !!!
DO YOU HAVE A VAGUE IDEA OF THE SUFFERING YOU FORCE ME TO ???

I FELT UNDESCRIBLE PAIN.
THE FROST BREAKING MY MUSCLES...
YET, THOSE WERE NOT AS PAINFUL AS GETTING BACK THAT NIGHT'S MEMORIES...
REMEMBERING MY CHRISTINE CALLING FOR HELP, BEGGING FOR MERCY, AND BEING VIOLATED WHILE HER FUTURE HUSBAND WAS BEATED TO DEATH, WAS TERRIBLE!
DON'T FORGET, PETER, I GAVE YOU IMMORTALITY AND INVINCIBILITY... IN OTHER WORDS I GAVE YOU ALL YOU NEED TO GET YOUR REVENGE!!!
BUT IT CAME WITH A PRICE... THE PRICE OF AN ETERNAL AGONY, OF AN ENLESS RAIN DURING A NIGHT WITH NO TOMORROW!

Stop the rain
Hot Play

If I loose myself tonight,
only Moon brush against,
in the crease of my mind.
Cold water cleans the stars,
falling down on my face,
swallow salt and bitter dust.
Disappear from view,
vanishing in the faded lights.
Fusion between opposed.

Please stop the rain...
Please stop the rain...

The rain...
Rolling tears streaming down,
drawing all your own face,
and drops bits and dance with you.
In the darkness of my dreams,
only light of you will stay...
I would be, be like the rain...
Oh, oh...
Waiting for the bite,
of the Midnight city life,
exhaust ourselves like dreams.

Please stop the rain...
Please stop the rain...
Please stop the rain...

NO RAIN WILL LAST FOREVER. AND THE NIGHT WILL ALWAYS BE FOLLOWED BY THE DAY, EVEN WHEN THE SUN WON'T CHASE THE DARKNESS AWAY.
IT MIGHT TAKES WEEKS... MONTHS... YET SOONER OR LATER THE SUN WILL COME BACK HIGH IN THE SKY... EVEN THOUGH IT'S NOT SURE TO SHINE FOR EVERYONE!!!

THE RECORD LABEL DID AN EXCEPTIONAL JOB. OUR SONG SOUNDS AMAZING...
YOU ARE A FLOWER AMONG THE FLOWERS.

TOC
TOC
KLAUS?

COME FORWARD!!!
WHAT THE HE...

STUMP!

QUICK, QUICK!
ALRIGHT, ALRIGHT...
JUST A MOMENT TO HAVE FUN
WITH THIS IDIOT!!!

AAHHRGH!
SHMP!

DONE! NOW WE CAN GO!

WROOOOM!!

ONE HOUR LATER...
DID YOU DO EXACTLY AS I ORDERED? DID ANYONE SEE WHAT HAPPENED?
NO WORRIES, DOCUPIL IS SAFE AND SOUND.

ALL AS ESTABILISHED. A LADY DID SEE US... AND KLAUS DOCUPIL'S CAR IS PARKED IN FRONT OF HER HOUSE.
WHAT'S NEXT?

NOTHING! ABSOLUTELY NOTHING!!! LET THE NEWS OF THE KIDNAPPING SPREAD AND THE DEAD COME TO ME! THIS TIME I WILL SEND IT TO HELL FOREVER!!!

CHRISTINA?!? YOU... HERE???
YES, PETER!!! I NEEDED TO SEE YOU...
IT'S ONLY A DREAM OF COURSE...
STILL, IT FEELS GREAT, DOESN'T IT?
DREAMS DO END, CRI...
TRUE, BUT IN YOUR DREAMS EVERYTHING IS BEAUTIFUL, MY LOVE, AND MAGICAL.

CRISTINA...
MY TRUE LOVE!
MY LIFE!!!
BEEING WITH YOU IS THE ONLY
THING I WOULD WISH FOR!

I MISS YOUR HANDS...
YOUR BODY...
YOUR LIPS SO MUCH!

IT'S AMAZING, CRISTINA, YOU ARE RIGHT!
IT'S JUST A DREAM, YET IT FEELS SO INCREDIBILY REAL!
SUBLIME PLEASURE!

I WILL KILL MICHELE, CRISTINA. AND I WILL KILL HIM IN A TERRIBLE WAY.
THEN AN ARID ETERNITY WILL WELCOME ME...
IN WHICH I WILL HAVE TO DO DISPICABLE THINGS TO RELIEVE THE PAIN...
IS IT ANY DIFFERENT??? LIFE LEFT MY BODY.
I HAVE NO SOUL. I AM COLD, I AM ONLY DEATH! DEATH, DEATH, DEATH!!!
THE FLAME OF OUR LOVE BURNED INTENSELY. AND IT WAS WONDERFUL. BUT IT IS NOT SAID THAT AN OLD FLAME CANNOT BURN AGAIN.
IT'S YOUR NEW NATURE, MY LOVE! EVEN FIERCE BEASTS KILL TO SURVIVE. BUT UNLIKE THEM... YOU CAN CHOOSE THOSE TO KILL!
YOU ARE ALIVE, PETER! YOUR HEART STILL BEATS! AND EVEN IF A DIFFERENT FATE AWAITS US, EACH OF US MUST GO ON.
BECAUSE YOU ARE REALLY DEAD, WHEN YOU BECOME UNABLE TO LOVE!

BACK TO THE NIGHTMARE AFTER THE MOST BEAUTIFUL DREAM...

WHERE IS HE?
I WAS WAITING FOR YOU, PETER! WHAT TOOK YOU SO LONG?

IF YOU ARE WONDERING ABOUT YOUR FRIEND KLAUS, WELL ... I'M TAKING CARE OF HIM WITH ALL THE LOVE I'M CAPABLE OF!

SO, TRY TO MOVE AND I'LL FILL YOU WITH LEAD!!!

LET'S GO GUYS!!! LET'S KILL THIS PIECE OF SHIT!!!

SON OF A BITCH, IT'S A TRAP!
ZACK!!!

ZACK!!!

POOR BASTARD! DID YOU REALLY THINK I WOULD FACE A VAMPIRE ONLY WITH THIS???

YOU ARE NOT INVINCIBLE AND YOU SIGNED YOUR SENTENCE TO DEATH THE DAY YOU STOLE MY WOMAN! MICHELE ABATE'S WOMAN!!!
ZACK!!!

CRISTINA WAS NO LONGER YOURS!!! SHE LEFT YOU!!! SHE REALIZED THAT YOU WERE THE BIGGEST MISTAKE OF HER LIFE!

SHUT UP, BASTARD!!! YOU TOOK HER AWAY FROM ME!!! HOW DID YOU DARE!!! I SHOULD HAVE KILLED YOU THE VERY SAME DAY YOU TOUCHED HER BODY!!
PAFFF!!

IMMOBILIZE THIS WORM AND GO GET THE OTHER ONE!!! BEFORE SENDING HIM BACK TO HELL, I WANT TO LOOK AT HIS FACE WHILE HE SEES HIS BEST FRIEND DYING!!! YES, HIS GIRLFRIEND'S BROTHER!!!

STUMP!
STUMP!
STUMP!

STUMP!
STUMP!
STUMP!
STUMP!
YOU LOST, UGLY PIECE OF SHIT! THEY ALL DO TO MICHELE ABATE!!! ASH WOOD... MORE LETHAL FOR YOU THAN A MACHINE GUN... ISN'T IT RIDICULOUS???
WE COULDN'T FIND HIM BOSS!!! KLAUS DOCUPIL IS GONE!!!

WHAT DO YOU MEAN HE'S GONE????? YOU IDIOTS!!!

VRIIIII
VRIIIII
VRIIIII
VRIIIII
VRIIIII
VRIIIII
VRIIIII
VRIIIII
VRIIIII
VRIIIII
I'M SORRY FOR YOU, PETER... BUT IT LOOKS LIKE YOU ARE GOING TO DIE ALONE!!! NO WORRIES THOUGH, KLAUS WILL JOIN YOU SOON!!!

VRiiii
VR VRiiii VR
VR VR VRiiii
VR VR
VRiiiii
WHAT THE HELL IS GOING ON???
VRiiii
VRii
VRiiii
ZACKiii
AHHRGH

AHHRGH!

CK!!!

NOOOOOOOO!!!

AHHRGH!
STUMP!

YOU CAN'T PASS THROUGH HER!

YOUR TIME HAS COME, UGLY SON OF BITCH!!!

COME ON, ASSHOLE...
GO ON AND KILL ME!!!

NO, MICHELE ABATE, NOT YET!
IT WILL BE OVER WHEN I SAY SO!!!
IT'S NOT OVER BETWEEN US UNTIL I SAY SO. YOU STILL LOVE ME... YOU NEVER STOPPED!

IT WILL BE OVER...
...WHEN...
...I SAY SO!!!

...I SAY SO!!!
...I SAY SO!!!

NOOOOOOO!!! PETEEEEEEER!!!
LEAVE ME ALONE! NO!!!
STOP IT! LET ME GO!!! PETER NEEDS ME!!! PLEASE, STOP!

IT WILL BE OVER WHEN I SAY SO!!!

YOUR PAIN WILL STOP ONLY WHEN I SAY SO!!!

YOU SHOULD STOP SAVING ME ... OR IT COULD BECOME A FULL-TIME JOB FOR YOU.

NO PROBLEM. I HAVE NOTHING BETTER TO DO FOR ALL OF *ETERNITY.*
IS KLAUS SAFE?
I'M HERE, PETER!

I'M SORRY, MY FRIEND. I WANTED TO TELL YOU EVERYTHING AT THE RIGHT TIME... BUT... THAT'S LIFE *!!!*

AAAAAAAAHHHHHH!!!!!!
AHHRGH!
STUMP!
YOU BASTARD!
STUMP!

AAAAHHHHHH

AAAAHHHHHH
I'LL MAKE YOUR FACE UNRECOGNIZABLE TO MATCH THE MONSTER YOU ARE!
I AM ONLY SORRY THAT YOU WILL NEVER BE ABLE TO SEE YOURSELF IN A MIRROR... AND FEEL THE SAME DISGUST I FEEL WHEN I LOOK AT YOU, YOU HORRIBLE PIECE OF SHIT!

NGH!!

AAAAHHHHHH
STRAAAPP

KRATCH
TRY NOT TO DIE, MICHELE ABATE! NOT SOON AT LEAST! I'LL BE BACK LOOKING FOR YOU SOON. UNTIL THEN IT WON'T BE OVER YET !!!

A FEW WEEKS LATER...
"YOU WERE RIGHT, CRISTINA! IT'S ONLY WHEN YOU BECOME UNCAPABLE TO LOVE, THAT YOU'RE REALLY DEAD."

"LOVE ISN'T THE ONLY THING YOU TAUGHT ME, THOUGH..."

I'LL BE BACK SOON, GIADA! I HAVE A VERY IMPORTANT APPOINTMENT TO ATTEND!

"I WILL TREASURE YOUR TEACHINGS, CRISTINA..."

AHHRGH!

NOW THAT YOU EXPERIENCED PAIN, MICHELE ABATE, I CAN SAY IT'S OVER!!!
CRACK

"VERY TRUE, CRISTINA ... I AM LIKE A FIERCE BEAST... FORCED TO KILL IN ORDER TO SURVIVE..."
"BUT, AS YOU SAID, UNLIKE THEM...

YES, OF COURSE! THIS CELL PHONE IS ONLY ONE OF THE MANY THINGS I WILL GIVE YOU... IF YOU DO JUST ONE THING FOR ME IN RETURN...

"I CAN CHOOSE...
...WHOM TO KILL!!!!"
THE END.